HIPPO LEAVES HOME

Roger Hargreaves

Publishers · GROSSET & DUNLAP · New York

Library of Congress Catalog Card Number: 81-84546
ISBN: 0-448-12317-7

First published in Great Britain by Hodder and Stoughton.
Published in the United States by Ottenheimer Publishers, Inc.
Published simultaneously in Canada.

HIPPO LEAVES HOME

One Saturday, two weeks ago, and nine hundred and ninety-nine miles from where you're reading this book, three people were asleep in Christmas Cottage.

Hippo, Potto, and young Mouse. Hippo was the first to wake up.

"Oh, look at the time," he cried, leaping out of bed. "I'm going to be late for work!"

But then he stopped. And thought. And smiled. So he got dressed and went downstairs to make breakfast for Potto and Mouse.

"Silly me," he giggled, "it's Saturday, and I don't have to go to work."

Hippo was drinking the very last drop of his coffee, and Mouse was nibbling the very last piece of his toast, when Potto arrived downstairs for breakfast. Looking very smart. "It's my new jacket," he said, turning around so that it could be admired.
Mouse grinned.
Hippo
groaned.

"Hippo," complained Potto, "this boiled egg is hard!"
Hippo sighed and boiled Potto another egg.
"And the toast is cold!"
Hippo sighed and toasted Potto another slice.
"And I hate to mention it, but this coffee is cold as well!"
Hippo sighed and made Potto some fresh coffee.
Just like Potto!

"Well," said Hippo after breakfast, "since today is Saturday, and we have nothing else to do, we could do some gardening!"

"Gardening?" squeaked Mouse.

"Me?" said Potto. "Garden?"

"Well, what else are you going to do today?" asked Hippo.

"Homework," replied Mouse quickly.

"This and that," replied Potto vaguely.

Hippo sighed.

Potto sat watching Hippo.
"How about a glass of
lemonade?" he called.
Hippo stopped gardening.
"That would be nice."
"It would," said Potto.
"Could you bring
mine out to me
here!"
Just like Potto.

Hippo cooked lunch for Potto and Mouse,
and washed up after Potto and Mouse,
and made Potto and Mouse's beds.
And then when Potto and Mouse had gone out for
a walk, Hippo sat down to think.
"I'm going to teach that lazy Potto and that
greedy Mouse a lesson," he thought.
And thought and thought.
And then he smiled.

When Potto and
Mouse arrived
home they were
hungry after
their walk.
"Hippo,"
boomed Potto
as they came in
through the door,
"any chance of a
hot buttered muffin
or two for tea?"
No reply!
"Covered with lovely
sticky strawberry
jam," added Mouse
hopefully.
No reply!
"Where is he?"
grumbled Potto.

Hippo had gone away.
While the other two
were out for their
walk, he'd packed
his suitcase and left.

And Potto and Mouse were left to look after themselves.
"That shouldn't be any problem," said Potto.
"Of course not," agreed Mouse.
But that Saturday night, because neither of them could cook, they went to bed hungry.
And miserable!

On Sunday, Potto decided it was time he learned to cook.
"We'll have roast beef and roast potatoes and peas,"
he announced grandly. "And gravy,"
he added as an afterthought.
"Ooo, Sunday lunch," squeaked
Mouse. "Super!"
But could Potto
cook Sunday lunch?
What do you think?
So again they went
to bed hungry
and miserable, in
their lumpy
unmade beds.

On Monday, neither of them woke up on time.
And Mouse was very late for school.
And got into trouble.

On Tuesday, Potto tried to light a fire.
But got himself, and Mouse, covered with soot!

On Wednesday, Mouse tried his hand at making a pie.
But got himself, and Potto, covered with flour!

On Thursday, Hippo telephoned. "How are you getting along without me?" he asked.

"Fine," lied Potto.
But Mouse grabbed the telephone.
"Oh, Hippo," he cried, "please come
home and look after us.
We're cold and we're hungry and
we promise to be good and to
help you.
We'll clean up
and make
our beds and
not complain
if only you'll
come home!"
Hippo smiled
to himself.
"Very well," he
said, "but
only if you do
all the things
you promise."
"Oh, yes, yes,
yes!" cried
Potto and
Mouse
together.

"Well, well," said Hippo,
when he saw the mess in
the living room.
"Well, well, well," said
Hippo, when he saw the
mess in the kitchen.
"Well, well, well, well,"
said Hippo, when he saw
the mess in the bedrooms.
"Well, well, well, well,
well," said Hippo, when
he saw the mess
in the bathroom.

The following morning, Friday, Potto and Mouse got out of bed when Hippo told them to.

And Mouse went off to school without making a fuss.

And Potto helped Hippo clean up.

And Potto even actually made his own bed.

And when Mouse came home from school, he did his homework without a murmur.

Hippo was very happy.

"Life is going to be very different at Christmas Cottage from now on," he thought. "Now that Potto and Mouse have changed their ways."

The day after was
Saturday again.
"Hippo," said Potto
at breakfast, "this
boiled egg is hard!"
"And the toast is cold!"
complained Mouse.
"And the coffee is cold, too,"
they added.
Poor Hippo sighed. He boiled
another egg, toasted more
toast, and made some fresh
coffee.

"Actually," said Potto, looking at his boiled egg and his hot toast and his fresh coffee, "actually, it's not what I feel like having for breakfast anyway. Can I have some cornflakes?"
Oh, dear!
Oh, Potto!